GIRL UNDER GRAIN

By

Karen Hartman

NoPassport Press
Dreaming the Americas Series

NoPassport Press
Dreaming the Americas Series
First edition 2010 by NoPassport Press
PO Box 1786, South Gate, CA 90280 USA; -
NoPassportPress@aol.com

ISBN: 978-0-578-04981-6

No Passport is a Pan-American theatre alliance & press devoted to live, virtual and print action, advocacy, and change toward the fostering of cross-cultural diversity in the arts with an emphasis on the embrace of the hemispheric spirit in US Latina/o and Latin-American theatre-making.

NoPassport Press' Theatre & Performance PlayTexts Series and its Dreaming the Americas Series promotes new writing for the stage, texts on theory and practice, and theatrical translations.

Contents

Thicker than blood, longer than birth:
Mother and Other
in Karen Hartman's *Girl Under Grain*

Here are some things I began to believe:
Work is thicker than blood.
Years are longer than birth.
And you can find another mother.

Karen Hartman designates *Girl Under Grain* a "dust bowl love story" inspired by the Book of Ruth. Beautifully written, incandescent and unflinching, it begins with a lone voice counting the lessons of her life: belief, work, years, and rebirth in the wake of loss. You can find another mother. You can transcend your circumstances.

The puzzle of the play begins. The Book of Ruth tells the story of Naomi, who is left without kin when her sons die. Her daughter-in-law, the Moabite Ruth, cleaves to her and accompanies Naomi back to her home with a pledge of fealty:

4

"…whither thou goest I will go; and where thou lodgest I will lodge; thy people shall be my people and thy God my God." (Ruth 1:14-16)

On the one hand Ms. Hartman delivers a provocative contribution to midrash (ancient commentary on Biblical texts); she reads between the lines of the Book of Ruth. The play becomes part of a tradition of commentary and interpretation in which the reader contemplates the text, fleshes out the events, and asks questions to uncover what lies beneath. But by merging the biblical journey with the dust bowl migration, Hartman not only breathes life into an ancient text, but also spins a wrenching, original American story of love found, lost, and found again. She poses questions: What if Ruth's supposed selflessness actually masked erotic desire? What if the older woman, Sugar (Naomi), returned this love? What if this passion, and not a baby, was the older woman's late life miracle? What if this love between abandoned women occurred in a time of catastrophic hardship where a woman's only chance to survive was to find a man to take her in? How would this story end?

Ruth is the rogue element in both *Girl Under Grain* and the Bible. Ruth enters a world where she does not belong and changes it. In the Bible, Ruth is absorbed into the tradition, becoming the first convert to Judaism. She gives birth to Obed, the grandfather of King David. In Hartman's world, it is the road, and not Boone's (Boaz's) farm, where Ruth and Sugar are the closest. As in King Lear, the great wilderness is the only place these women's souls are free. Each woman leaps away from everything she has known life to be. And the tension Hartman creates around how differently the women behave when they arrive at Boone's farm and become subject to societal conventions is the awful motor of the action.

When I directed *Girl Under Grain*, I was stunned by the contrasting journeys of Hartman's three nomadic women, Ruth, Sugar, and Orpah. Hartman is not interested in documenting what women's lives actually were like in the dust bowl, but rather in exposing the choices women are forced to make in order to survive. We are asked to witness, not to take sides. Hartman is interested in how circumstance and intention make us who we are. What we do to ensure our physical survival often comes at untenable psychic expense. Sugar, now in her 50's, employs wisdom, charm, and wariness to hold a hostile world at bay. Ruth, who lost her mother at an early age, is tough and eager to take care of others, sometimes at her own expense. Orpah, the youngest, is a self-styled princess on a pea. She trades on her looks to get where she wants to go. These choices are ferociously important to Hartman; they can lead to love, loss, triumph, shame, or most likely, some alloy thereof.

Girl Under Grain is brilliantly structured. Hartman creates her own spare language with words as plain and lonely as the objects in a Walker Evans WPA photo. The play begins in the midst of catastrophe—three women trudging down a dusty road after their men and car have disappeared. Ruth chooses to stick with her mother-in-law, and soon after Sugar goes blind. Ruth's devotion is expressed through small things—carving a stick so Sugar can walk with dignity, giving Sugar all of the coffee, washing Sugar's hair. The dazzling contrast between the two women in this intergenerational love story renders it even more believable, tragicomic, and moving. Crustiness is answered with compassion: *I don't like you, Ruth,* Sugar says. Ruth responds: *I'll stick.*

The miracle Hartman embeds in *Girl Under Grain* is simply this: love is sudden, powerful, and can transform you. A sensuous passion blossoms between unlikely partners on the road between sea and farm, between present and the past. Hartman creates a wide world where no one sees; it is here the women can share who they are and *see* each other. Consider the exchange below:

Sugar: Head bent. Eyes blank. Skin slack. Tits gray. Feet full of pus.

Ruth: I imagine I can touch you.

Sugar: Well. That's something. To love a Broken person. That's kind.

Ruth: You are the most beautiful part of my eye

The dustbowl evokes both the baleful event in American history, and Sugar's pelvis, her lost fertility. Ruth seeks in Sugar the mother she's lost. She apes Sugar's stoic traditions and studies Sugar's confidence and heartfelt prayer. Sugar sees in Ruth the fertility she can bring to Boone, the child that will redeem her losses and bring Sugar back into her inheritance.

Karen Hartman has said that in her plays she likes to place private moments in public so that people don't feel so alone. *Girl Under Grain* is a play of highly intimate moments counterpointed by songs. We see a woman go blind; hear a declaration of animal attraction; watch two women lie down to make love; eavesdrop on a hitchhiker singing in the back of a truck; listen to Boone on his porch proclaim his power to the wide world; witness a seduction and a consummation on the threshing floor; hear the screams of Ruth laboring to give birth, alone; see a dried up old woman nurse a newborn; observe a strip tease artist being humiliated by a stage hand; and finally watch Ruth, in sailor whites, walk into the sea. *Girl Under Grain* multiplies the private moments until they outweigh the public ones. And when Ruth reclaims her life, when she has given birth and realizes than Sugar will never

let Ruth love her the way she did on the road,
she picks up her bag to go and says about her
baby:

I don't want to know his name. Don't tell him
mine.
Keep him warm. Keep him safe. If that's possible.
Tell him, you are a child of desire. You better watch
what you want.

In performance the sequence of scenes on the
farm reaches Artaudian cruelty. Sugar's
repeated fearful denials of Ruth, Ruth and
Boone's devouring each other in the barn, and
Sugar and Boone singing songs while Ruth's
ragged birthing screams emerge from the
house are excruciating to witness. The
audience feels complicit, engaged in the cruelty
of repression, and subtly but viscerally
Hartman makes her point. How could such a
rare love be so quickly abandoned? Why are
we afraid of our erotic desires? What does it
mean to be foreign? To be other? To be, as
Ruth puts it in the final line of the play,
"something else?"

I would be remiss to close without saluting the
producers, designers, and actors who helped

bring *Girl Under Grain* into the world. Roger Danforth at the Drama League gave us a berth in the 1998 New Directors/New Works program, and then presented us in the New York International Fringe Festival in August 2000. *Girl Under Grain* won "Best Drama" in the festival. Antonio Sacre, in *Theatre Reviews Limited*, observed, "Complicated, poetic and beautiful, the writing and acting are thrilling to watch. Dale Soules is some kind of wonderful, a salt of the earth, powerful woman who finds humor and pain in seemingly every phrase....And Sibyl Kempson more than holds her own with her; she manages to slide into the many complexities of the dialogue with the ease of a stream gently eroding away a river bank..." I would like to thank Mike Hodge, Nina Landey, Mandy Fox, and Kristin DiSpaltro for their equally stunning work, and P73 Productions for extending the Fringe run. Matthew Adelson created evocative lighting. Aaron Hartman and Kim Sherman made the songs sing; Tim Cusak writing for NYTheatre.com noted, "I want a recording of Aaron Hartman's songs for the next time my heart gets broken." Geoff Zink designed the sound around early twentieth century slide guitar riffs. More than anything I remember

11

how actors and designers created richness out of spareness, just as Ruth and Sugar and their Biblical forebears had done before them.

Jean Randich
New York City, 2000

Girl Under Grain

by

Karen Hartman

a dust bowl love story

inspired by the Book of Ruth

Girl Under Grain

Characters:

Ruth   A woman from near the ocean.
        Thirty.

Orpah   From the same place. Twenties.

Sugar   A woman from solid land.
        Mother-in law to Ruth and
        Orpah. Fifties.

Boone   A prosperous farmer. Fifties.

Setting:

Part One   A road.

Part Two   Boone's large farm.

Epilogue   An establishment near the ocean.

Overlapping text is indicated by an asterisk (*)
at the place where the second line begins, for
example:
SUGAR: Your faithful loving ones, Mother and
Orpah *and Ruth.

RUTH: What?

Girl Under Grain was first produced by the Drama League at the New York International Fringe Festival, August 17, 2000.

It was awarded "Best Drama" in the festival, and extended by P73 Productions at the Clemente Soto Vélez Cultural Center on September 9, 2000.

It was directed by Jean Randich; the set design was by Ms. Randich; the costume design was by the company; the lighting design was by Matthew Adelson; the sound design was by Geoff Zink; the assistant director and stage manager was Rebecca Viale. The composer was Aaron Hartman. Boone's Lullaby was composed by Kim D. Sherman.

The cast was as follows:

Ruth – Sibyl Kempson
Orpah – Kristin DiSpaltro
Sugar – Dale Soules
Boone – Mike Hodge

Girl Under Grain was developed through the Drama League's New Directors/New Works Project in 1998, with the same company, except Nina Landey as Ruth, Mandy Fox as Orpah, and composition by Kim D. Sherman.

Girl Under Grain received a new play commission from the National Foundation for Jewish Culture. It was supported by workshops at the Playwrights Center, Center Stage, A.S.K. Theater Projects, the Bay Area Playwrights Festival, and the Streisand Festival of New Jewish Plays.

Girl Under Grain cover photo: Daniel Shiffman. Courtesy of P73 Productions.

In memory of Gertie Rodd
(1908-2004)

.

GIRL UNDER GRAIN

PROLOGUE

RUTH or RUTH'S VOICE:
Here are some things I began to believe:
Work is thicker than blood.
Years are longer than birth.
And you can find another mother.

PART ONE

One

America. A time of migration.

Three women walk along a road: ORPAH, SUGAR, then RUTH. Orpah is in her twenties; Sugar is in her fifties; Ruth is thirty. They wear cotton dresses and carry bundles and bags. Orpah and Ruth wear men's shoes.

The women are walking east. Cars are moving west. They walk a while.

ORPAH: Ow.

They walk.

OW.

They walk.

ORPAH (CONT): **MY FOOT HURTS!**

SUGAR: Stuff the toe.

ORPAH: I did.

SUGAR: Make a callous.

ORPAH: Can't.

SUGAR: Walk on.

ORPAH: I will age and die on this road. My feet will splay like old claws. It is unnatural for a girl to wear these boots.

SUGAR: Unnatural? Unnatural is falling to sleep surrounded by sons and waking up with their wives.

ORPAH: Where did he go? When will he appear?

SUGAR: Keep an eye out for bodies torn by beasts.
ORPAH: We will find our men!

SUGAR: Sure, with them strewn god knows where and us making record time.

ORPAH: Why can't I wear my own shoes?

SUGAR: Because they are ridiculous.

ORPAH: She called us ridiculous!

A small painful pause.

RUTH: I... I...

ORPAH: A STONE. See? I told you his goddamn shoe cut my goddamn ankle every step, the right one worse. See? I told you I had hot spots this morning under all that weight. Now they're big packs of pus.
Anyone got a pin?

SUGAR: Stand up and walk.

Orpah removes a pin from her hat and starts popping her blisters.

ORPAH: OOOH. AHHH. OOOH. YESSSSS.

She offers the pin to Ruth.

ORPAH (CONT): You want to try? If I had a piece of stocking I could slip it over my foot and then I'd slide by the rough spots in this damn shoe. Anyone got a stocking left? A sock?

Ruth: I HAVE A SOCK.

RUTH FINDS ONE SOCK.

It's clean.

ORPAH: What I can do is switch this sock from foot to foot and increase my endurance.

RUTH: Or you can wear it on one foot only and always have a place free of pain.

ORPAH: Or I can split this sock down the center and –

SUGAR: My son's corpses could be anywhere on earth.

ORPAH: Hope the corpses enjoy our car and my last money.

SUGAR: Girls. You have a home. Go there. To be honest, we're not related anymore. I brought my sons west to find work and they found you. To be honest, I feel better with my back to the sea. I used to watch the land expand in all directions, but now there are just two. Front and back. You aren't getting younger, either one. Go home and wash the dirt from the folds in your skin. Braid your hair. Try to have a baby. To be honest, it's your best chance at love.

ORPAH: Okay.

Orpah opens the smallest suitcase, changes into battered pumps and the single sock, and steps into the road, hitching glamorously. A car slows right away.

ORPAH (CONT): HELLO.

SUGAR: Kiss me goodbye.

Orpah does. Tender. The car honks.

ORPAH: *(TO RUTH)* Come with me.

SUGAR: Kiss me goodbye.

RUTH: Oh.

ORPAH: Come on.

RUTH: I—

ORPAH: We'll ride back to the coast with our feet up. Easy. One long strip of road. Easy. A new beginning for you and me.

RUTH: I want to stay.

ORPAH: Stay where?

Car honks again.

RUTH: Don't miss your ride.

ORPAH: I'm going to live in a big big place with men wrapped around me like a coat.

Orpah steps into the car. It drives away.

SUGAR: Catch up to them.

RUTH: It's a car.

SUGAR: Wave him down.

RUTH: Go! Go! Go!

SUGAR: *(To car)* Stay!

RUTH: *(To Sugar)* Okay.

Before you cry you clear a place for yourself in the dirt. You lay down a cloth. You sit. You

RUTH (CONT): wait three breaths before releasing a single sob or drop.

SUGAR: How have you spent your time?

RUTH: You always know what a person will say, what they will eat. You make up a bed before we're tired. I swear I would forget about darkness each morning and sunrise every night, without you.

SUGAR: You're not old yet. Find someone nice.

RUTH: Don't try to split off.
I will go with you.
Rest with you.
Worship and die with you.
I watch you walk and I think there's a God.
I want to carry myself like that, and if I have to carry you I can.
Lightning rip me in two if I'm telling a lie.

SUGAR: I don't like you, Ruth.

RUTH: I'll stick.

Two

The hot middle of the day.

Sugar and Ruth are walking east.

RUTH: From behind, her legs are two small animals. Separate, lumbering, strange and strong.

SUGAR: Did you hear about the farmer's wife who ran away?
He tractor.
Why did the rooster chase the acrobat hen?
She flew the loop.
What did the grasshopper say to the crow?

RUTH: Let's go against the grain.

They laugh. Sugar falls.

RUTH (CONT): I've never seen the top of your head.

SUGAR: Don't get old.

RUTH: What tripped you?

SUGAR: I forgot to look.

RUTH: Get up.

SUGAR: I am.

RUTH: Get up.

SUGAR: I will.

Silence.

RUTH: How many fingers?

Two.

SUGAR: Three.

RUTH: You went blind and I missed it.

SUGAR: I didn't look.

RUTH: You tripped on plain ground.

SUGAR: Goddamn shoes.

RUTH: How many arms? How many breasts? How many women?

SUGAR: Two.

Ruth holds Sugar.

Three

Evening.

Ruth has a long branch and a small knife. She hacks off the cross branches. She chips away at one end of the stick to make a point. The knife slips.

RUTH: MAAA!

Ruth licks her wound.

Four

Night.

Sugar holds the stick. She waves it in front of her like a baton or a sword. She slams it into the ground. She holds it straight out in both hands and whirls around and around. She falls.

SUGAR: *(Calling over distance)* Ruth!

RUTH: *(There the whole time)* Yes?

Sugar slowly pulls herself up with the stick.

SUGAR: Which way is straight?

Ruth sets Sugar facing east. They walk very slowly in the darkness.

As they go:

A

Orpah sings to herself in the back of a bumpy truck.

ORPAH: *Now I groan, all alone*
Now I cry and sigh and fly each night away
To the sky in my eye
Where the rising moon don't chase the sun away.

I'm a lonely girl
Moving in the world
My mom, my man, my plans fade in the road.
I'm the only girl
You've noticed in the world
So slow your car and roll away my load.

Oh my skin is my kin
And my hands and feet I greet like company
But my heart is the part
That did hop a fence and run away from me.

I'm a lonely girl
Moving in the world
My body is the only place I know.
I'm the only girl
Remaining in the world
I'll ride along as far as you will go.

Five

Morning. Ruth makes coffee over a fire. Sugar sits.

SUGAR: What's burning?

RUTH: Coffee.

SUGAR: Why you burning it?

RUTH: I made a fire.

SUGAR: FIRE?

RUTH: It's safe.

SUGAR: Don't burn my coffee.

RUTH: I won't, Ma.

SUGAR: If I was your Ma, I'd a taught you how to make coffee.

RUTH: I make it the way I do.

SUGAR: You were eight?

When she died.

RUTH: Yeah.

SUGAR: That's old enough.

RUTH: Do you want the coffee?

SUGAR: Maybe she was thinking, nine. Nine is a better age to handle hot things. It's a

SUGAR (CONT): tragedy. You making bad coffee the rest of your life.

RUTH: Because it's ready.

SUGAR: What did it feel like?

RUTH: I don't remember. Bad.

SUGAR: Maybe if you lose a lot early on it gets easy.

RUTH: I don't think so.

SUGAR: I hoped my sons would learn from the weather. Freeze and thaw. Fall and sprout. Plant and reap. But to be honest they never showed too much perspective.

RUTH: Here.

Sugar drinks.

SUGAR: Too sweet.

RUTH: I gave you our last sugar.

SUGAR: It's sweet.

RUTH: You like it sweet.

SUGAR: I don't.

RUTH: You take two big spoons.

SUGAR: I'm poor and I'm female and everyone's dead. Why sugar up my drink? I'll take it black.

Sugar dumps out the coffee.

RUTH: I like a little sweet.

SUGAR: More please.

RUTH: You think I have endless everything.

SUGAR: Now is my time of loss. I need coffee how I like it.

RUTH: Okay.

Ruth pours more coffee. Sugar drinks.

SUGAR: It's cold.

RUTH: It was hot.

SUGAR: Well isn't that a fact of science.

She drinks.

SUGAR (CONT): Bitter.

RUTH: I'll kill you.

SUGAR: Just joking. Have a little coffee, Ruthie. You act like a slug. Have a little heat.

RUTH: Okay.

Ruth fixes herself a cup.

SUGAR: Better?

RUTH: I guess. It's mostly grounds. I really only made two cups.

SUGAR: We are women drinking coffee on a lovely day.

Both sip. Luxurious.

RUTH: Tell me about sex.

SUGAR: I liked it.

RUTH: That's good.

More sipping. The distant sound of a car.

SUGAR: Heading east.

The car gets closer. Ruth jumps into the road and waves her arms around.

RUTH: Hey. HEY! Hey please? PLEASE?

The car honks. Ruth leaps out of the way so she doesn't get run over.

RUTH (CONT): Come back! COME BACK!

Car sounds fade away.

SUGAR: You don't have much of a way with men.

RUTH: Help me.

SUGAR: Oh, child.

RUTH: That's right.

SUGAR: We're going where you sweep your porch at dawn and it's clean all day.

RUTH: I would like a porch.

SUGAR: Poor baby.

RUTH: That's right.

SUGAR: Come here.

Ruth settles into Sugar's body.

SUGAR (CONT): You're going to like my friend Boone. Land cracks and he cracks back. Standing on the porch of his brittle home he will offer us water, some shade, whatever can be spared. He and I grew together like plants under green grass tall as a child. I keep that young land behind my eyes with my men and my old self. Together we will make a new farm. Our dusty shoes and empty sacks will overflow with rain. Next harvest there will be so much grain the men drop it as they go. You can gather and grind the extra and we will always eat. Then just when it's getting cold you can go to the big house and warm his feet with your belly and he will bless you and keep us for the rest of my life.

Sugar inhales deeply.

SUGAR (CONT): You smell bad.

RUTH: I know.

SUGAR: Me too.

RUTH: No point in washing to walk through dirt.

SUGAR: Let's pack it up, then.

RUTH: Okay.

Ruth bundles the supplies, helps Sugar up, and hands her the stick. They walk.

B

Orpah sits by the side of a road. She has a candy bar and a harmonica. She takes a small bite of the candy and experiments with the blues.

ORPAH:

I woke up this morning to reach for that man of mine.

Where his body oughta be was a paper he did sign:

Awful sorry baby, gone to join the railroad line.

He's flying high to find the sky

and send it home to me.

I walk to the store the way we used to go.

They got his meat and wine but I can't buy it, no.

I'm eating lean since my man joined the rodeo.

He's flying high to find the sky

and wrap it up for me.

On a windy night I hear his sweet guitar.

See him in the light of every passing car.

ORPAH (CONT): *I don't sleep right since my man became a movie star.*

He's flying high to find the sky

  and tear it down for me.

  He had to go, how could he know

I'm low as low can be.

More harmonica. Another careful bite of candy. Orpah turns toward the sound of a car.

Six

Day. Sugar and Ruth walk slowly, Sugar in front with her stick. Sugar dictates a letter.

SUGAR: We accept that animals have torn you up.

RUTH: Tore you up.

SUGAR: We pray for you in every step.

RUTH: You in every step.

SUGAR: We miss your long sure backs and your fixing hands.

RUTH: Hands.

SUGAR: We walk light on all ground in case it's your grave.

RUTH: Light on all ground in case it's *your grave.

SUGAR: Your faithful loving ones, Mother and Orpah *and Ruth.

RUTH: What?

SUGAR: In the miraculous event that you are not dead,

RUTH: Uh huh.

SUGAR: Stay the hell away from me and my bleeding feet. By the time we get home I'll be shoving stumps into your shoes and in no mind for a tender excuse. Find me a cure for blindness and age or don't find me at all. I plan to appear younger and more gorgeous than you ever saw me, and dead dead dead.

Walks.

Got that?

RUTH: Remember most of it.

SUGAR: Why have eyes and legs that work if all you do is remember? Write it down.

RUTH: I can't write when we're walking.

SUGAR: I walk. I don't see. I walk.

RUTH: I watch you.

SUGAR: Men were born to do one thing and then the next thing and then the next. Women do everything at once. That's the difference. Walk with your feet and brain; write with your hands and eyes.

RUTH: No.

SUGAR: Well.

RUTH: You need some attention. You fall down a lot.

SUGAR: When have you caught me?

RUTH: I make it so you don't trip as much.

SUGAR: From behind?

RUTH: Sometimes.

SUGAR: Well, stop. I don't want false pride. You go first, to hurry me up.

RUTH: No.

SUGAR: We move at the speed of a rock.

RUTH: I don't mind.

SUGAR: We're low on supplies.

RUTH: You can't tell what we have.

SUGAR: I know what they left.

Ruth: LIGHTNING RIP ME HAND FROM HAND. HIP FROM SHOULDER. EYE FROM EYE.

SUGAR: We're already cursed.

RUTH: I lied. I watch you because I like to. Because you are the most beautiful part of the road.

SUGAR: Don't joke.

RUTH: I imagine sometimes I can touch you.

SUGAR: Head bent. Eyes blank. Skin slack. Tits gray. Feet full of pus.

RUTH: I imagine I can touch you.

SUGAR: Well. That's something. To love a broken person. That's kind.

RUTH: You are the most beautiful part of my eye.

Sugar turns for the first time.

SUGAR: Where are you, Ruth?

RUTH: *(Touching Sugar)* Here. And here. And here.

SUGAR: You are a kind, kind, person.

RUTH: The thing is, I'm not.

SUGAR: You use your sight in a gentle way.

RUTH: I don't miss where I came from.

SUGAR: Good.

Silence.

RUTH: Can we stop and lie down?

SUGAR: Is it night?

RUTH: Sure.

SUGAR: Well then let's stop. And lie down.

RUTH: Okay.

Ruth lays Sugar down in a romantic way.

SUGAR:
Lay us down safely for one night.
Spread peace over us like wings.
Hide us against your heart that beats and
bleeds like mine.

<u>C</u>

Orpah sings to get warm.

ORPAH:
In the night, in the night
I'm a princess on a pea
Tiny stones
Bruise my bones
Breezes waken me.

In the night, in the night
Every pebble is a test
Can it be
Tender me
Never will find rest?

Somebody's child is lying awake
One young girl is cold
Uncover me
Discover me
Your mistake revealed in my ache
Food within the fold.

In the night, in the night
Tiny peas expand in rows
On the ground
Green and round

ORPAH (CONT): *Sleeping safe and close.*

 Now the night turns to white
Lights the shadow where I lay
Princess true
Black and blue
Walking one more day.

Seven

Bright morning.

SUGAR: COFFEE COFFEE COFFEE COFFEE COFFEE!

RUTH: Coming up.

SUGAR: It's our last cup, baby, make it good.

RUTH: How do you know?

SUGAR: Scraping the can. Wonder we got this far.

Ruth hands Sugar a cup. Sugar drinks.

RUTH: Mmm.

SUGAR: Where's yours?

RUTH: Drinking it. Tasty.

SUGAR: Show me your cup.

RUTH: I finished.

SUGAR: How dare you fool me?

RUTH: You love coffee.

SUGAR: I do.
Did I drink the whole can?

RUTH: Mostly.

Ruth and Sugar laugh.

SUGAR: Are you eating half?

RUTH: When I do.

SUGAR: You felt thin.

RUTH: Oh.

SUGAR: I want you to eat.

RUTH: It wasn't my dream.

SUGAR: Well, what did you dream?

RUTH: What did you dream?

SUGAR: Something real nice.

Quiet. The sound of a car going east.

Get him. Get him.

The car gets very loud, then passes.

RUTH: I want to stay.

SUGAR: On what? Stay on what?

RUTH: Just for one minute.

SUGAR: There will be minute after minute after minute. You stop the next car.

RUTH: Can I wash your hair?

SUGAR: I was that dirty?

RUTH: I'd like to. There's plenty of water, still warm.

SUGAR: Don't boil it.

RUTH: I won't.

SUGAR: You'll blister my head.

RUTH: You think so?

Ruth tests the water.

SUGAR: When you bathe a baby you heat the water till it feels like nothing. What's warm to me and you can burn a child. Same with my head.

RUTH: Do you trust my hands?

SUGAR: Yes.

RUTH: That's what I thought.

SUGAR: I used to rub the lambs and then myself for the way it felt soft. Your skin was a little like that.

RUTH: Your skin was like wet silk.

Ruth brushes water against Sugar's skin.

RUTH (CONT.): Is this right?

SUGAR: Yes.

Ruth strokes, combs and washes Sugar's hair.

D

Orpah slaps her thighs in rhythm. Loud sing-song.

ORPAH:
Feed me butter, feed me bread.
Set me up a mighty spread.
Give me coffee, give me meat
All the chickens I can eat.

Bake me up a cherry pie
Whipped cream, ice cream don't be shy.
Chocolate cake and lemon too
Then I'll know your love is true.

ONE TWO THREE FOUR
WON'T BE HUNGRY ANY MORE
FIVE SIX SEVEN EIGHT
I CAN CLEAN YOUR BIGGEST PLATE.

EIGHT SEVEN SIX FIVE
FEEDING KEEPS OUR LOVE ALIVE
FOUR THREE TWO ONE
WIPE MY MOUTH WHEN I GET DONE.

Eight

Evening into night. Ruth and Sugar are clean.

SUGAR: Still day?

RUTH: Cooling down.

SUGAR: We didn't budge.

RUTH: Sorry to waste your time.

SUGAR: Get my stick.

RUTH: Not at night.

SUGAR: I can walk.

RUTH: You got ants in your blood. Your whole family.

SUGAR: Say again?

RUTH: He didn't sleep one still night.

SUGAR: Nor as a boy.

RUTH: He regarded my body in a way I did not understand. He touched my breast like it was a miracle. That look on his face... remained a mystery for some time.

SUGAR: Where are you, Ruth?

RUTH: Here.

SUGAR: Do you look at me that way?

RUTH: Yes.

SUGAR: Forty years since I saw that look. Isn't life a silly story?

RUTH: I don't know.

SUGAR: My life has been filled with the silliest things. Here we are. Two clean-haired women sitting in the dirt. Oh boy.

Sugar begins to laugh.

SUGAR (CONT): Oh boy.

RUTH: Oh boy.

Ruth and Sugar laugh hard together.

SUGAR: Now I am laughing, I am laughing at the silly things I seen. How come you're laughing?

RUTH: I am just full of pleasure right now.

SUGAR: You are a blessing on my old bones.

RUTH: I am?

SUGAR: You make the sky rest softer on my face.

RUTH: Good.

SUGAR: Listen.

RUTH: What?

SUGAR: Heading east.

RUTH: No.

SUGAR: Listen.

The faint sound of a car.

RUTH: Oh yeah.

SUGAR: Let your hair loose and step into the road.

RUTH: Really?

SUGAR: Now.

Ruth does. The car approaches and stops. Bright truck lights in Ruth's face. Engine loud.

RUTH: My mother is blind and we have to go home.

Engine cuts out. In the headlights, Ruth gathers their things and takes Sugar by the hand. They step up into the lights.

End of Part One

PART TWO

One

Boone stands on his property. A large man,
Sugar's age. He wears work clothes. He chants to
the sky in a deep voice.

BOONE:
I look to the west and what do I see?
Sugar sugar lady riding home to me.
I look to the east and what do I know?
Sugar sugar lady don't have far to go.
I work every morning and I work at noon.
Work my hand to blisters for my sugar spoon.
I wait for an hour then I wait ten year...

Sees Sugar in the distance.

Sugar sugar lady is finally here.

That you, Sugar?
That you?
Last I saw you you were counting your cows,
counting up blades of grass. Last I saw you we
were nine, hunting buttercups in the snow.
Last I saw you you were in white and making
big plans. Last I saw you was the back of a

BOONE (CONT): yellow dress. The tail of a horse. And some dust.

That you? Standing before my farm? Sugar?

Sugar and Ruth appear in shadow.

SUGAR: It might be best to call me something else.

BOONE: Whatsa matter, lose your sweet ways?

SUGAR: May have.

BOONE: On your own. Everybody dead. Not too sugary a situation.

SUGAR: That's what I'm thinking.

BOONE: I named you for the taste of your fingers. The taste of your hair.

SUGAR: Well, you'll have to name me over. Road Dust. There's a good one. Age. Grief. Gray.

BOONE: Grain. Because you seem to think that you are your own little bit.

SUGAR: You sound like a satisfied man.

BOONE: I have rebuilt. Did you expect paint so white? Fields so even? But I guess you know about rich. You married rich. Rode after rich. Tried to buy your own skin brand new.

BOONE (CONT): Where's that gold, Sugar?
Where's the tree that never turns brown?
Breathe deep.

Sugar breathes.

SUGAR: You made it grow again.

BOONE: Look at me. Look at this old farm.
Look at me.

Sugar turns.

SUGAR: Boone.

BOONE: Oh, child.

SUGAR: Don't be cruel.

BOONE: You felt your way home.

SUGAR: I am a husk of a person. I make
empty, rattling sounds. I am an unloved
person.

BOONE: Who's the girl?

RUTH: I guess I don't know.

SUGAR: She married my youngest.

BOONE: Drove him off, huh?

RUTH: She said you were kind.

BOONE: Well how come you're not home with the oranges? With the grapes big as eyes? How come you're not riding the sea?

RUTH: I believe in family. I believe in places that make people like her.

BOONE: You must be a city girl.

RUTH: So?

BOONE: You're going to be real useful.

SUGAR: She has been good to me, Boone.

BOONE: That true?

RUTH: I love her.

BOONE: You love the unloved person. You must be real large. You must be worth a lot.

RUTH: Keep talking. I won't turn back.

BOONE: We'll clear a soft spot for you in the big house, Lady Grain. The foreign girl can sleep outdoors.

RUTH: We're used to that. Both of us.

SUGAR: Now Ruthie, I'm old. I take comfort where I can.

RUTH: You sure do.

Boone: I'll tell you what, Ruthie. This is my best harvest yet. I've got men working can't see to can't see and still my wheat goes on for miles. You walk along after them. What they forget, you remember. What they drop, you pick up. Then grind it and bake something nice.

Ruth stands still.

RUTH: I left a father, and a brother, and three cousins, and a bed just for me.

You better eat what I bring.

Ruth goes.

SUGAR: Still got my old checkerboard?

BOONE: I was using it for a table a while in there.

SUGAR: Wanna play?

BOONE: Lost the pieces.

SUGAR: Where could they go?

BOONE: It's a lot of property now.

SUGAR: How's our old place? How's my corn?

BOONE: I'll pour you some lemonade.

He does. She drinks.

BOONE (CONT): You like that?

SUGAR: What are they saying about me?

BOONE: Well, I don't imagine they're talking too favorably about your appearance. I don't imagine they are admiring that dress.

SUGAR: Are you married?

Boone extends his hand. She feels for a ring.

Big farmer like yourself.

BOONE: What happened to your eyes?

SUGAR: They failed. She cut me this stick. Who do you talk to, Boone? Being richer than everyone here?

BOONE: It is a solitary life.

Ruth walks by with a huge load of grain on her back.

BOONE: Strong girl.

SUGAR: Something else.

BOONE: Got a sack her own size.

SUGAR: She can do some things.

BOONE: Must be helpful.

SUGAR: You need a son.

BOONE: I got old, too.

SUGAR: My boys were the youngest, most powerful part of me. I used to watch those large males with my face and think, I could be tall. I could understand machines.

BOONE: Life takes a long time, don't you think?

SUGAR: There are surprises, Boone.

Quiet. Ruth walks by the other way, empty-handed.

BOONE: Child! Lemonade?

Ruth approaches the porch.

SUGAR: See how this one never sweats? Sit down, baby. Feel her face. Dry as silk.

Sugar reaches out and strokes Ruth's face.

RUTH: Oh.

BOONE: How's work?

RUTH: Real nice bunch a men you got there.

BOONE: They bothering you?

RUTH: I can take it.

Boone picks up a megaphone or cups his hands like one. Chant/speak.

BOONE:
This is Boone.
The richest man around.
This here is Boone.
I employ you.
This here is Boone.
The tallest horse, the brickest house, the shining machine.
This is Boone.
I tell you:
Leave the girl alone.
Leave that girl alone.
She is a new girl
Belonging to the lady we once called Sugar.
She is a strong girl.
I know she's there.
I know she's strange.
I say she can take what she like.
This here is Boone
To tell you hounds and free men:
Leave the girl alone.
Leave that girl alone.

Two

Night time. Ruth brings her bedding onto the porch. Inside the house, warm lights, low voices, and a phonograph.

RUTH: Lay her down safely tonight.
Spread peace like a shadowy wing.
Hide me inside her heart.
Make it beat with mine.
Make me a holy person
Without envy.

Ruth lies down, awake. After a time, Sugar walks onto the porch. She stands and breathes a while. She reaches out the way she stroked Ruth's face, then draws her hand in and strokes her own face. Sugar turns and goes inside, where the music and lights fade.

RUTH (CONT): Make me a substantial person
Without shame.

Three

Another day. Boone and Sugar play checkers with pennies and bottle caps.

SUGAR: King me.

BOONE: Can't.

SUGAR: I got to your side.

BOONE: My cap won't fit on your penny. No kings.

SUGAR: You have been a cheater your whole life.

BOONE: I cheated?

SUGAR: That was different.

BOONE: As a kid I thought it would hold. Destiny. Sugarfinger and me. I guess I was mixing up destiny and eternity.

SUGAR: Not a lot is forever.

BOONE: For example, your men are dead.

SUGAR: Yes they are.

BOONE: I'm rich.

SUGAR: Yes.

BOONE: And you got old.

SUGAR: Why do people love me in this bitter way? I want to be loved simply, without anger.

BOONE: You want a lot.

SUGAR: I had a wonderful marriage.

BOONE: Sing me a song about a wonderful marriage.

SUGAR: I can't.

BOONE: Precisely. Me, I have a taste for the dramatic. That's why I farm.

SUGAR: I wish my boys saw it that way.

BOONE: Well then why did you move them off their own property?

SUGAR: Not everyone is you.

BOONE: Remember that.

Ruth walks by with a huge load of grain. She has gotten stronger. She wears pants.

BOONE (CONT): Child!

Ruth looks up.

SUGAR: Hello, baby.

Ruth collapses under the grain. Boone goes to her.

BOONE: You are a wonderful worker.

He unburies her.

RUTH: I miss you.

Sugar goes into the house. Ruth waits three breaths, then starts to cry.

BOONE: Come eat something.

RUTH: Not hungry.

BOONE: You're turning into a bone. Come in the shade.

RUTH: Okay.

He leads her up to the porch.

BOONE: What's the matter with you? Have a little cake.

RUTH: No.

BOONE: I want you to drink a little lemonade. Good girl. Now one bite of cake. I can feed it to you. Good. A little lemonade. Mmm hmm. And some cake. Lemonade. Mmm hmm. And cake. Don't cry, child. It's just Boone being good to you. Cry later. Eat now.

Ruth starts to eat on her own.

BOONE (CONT): There you go.

Ruth eats the whole cake.

RUTH: I ate the whole cake.

BOONE: You had an appetite.

RUTH: I had an appetite for the whole cake.

BOONE: Your mother and I watch you working so hard.

RUTH: She doesn't watch me.

BOONE: But she would.

RUTH: Where did she go? What happened?

BOONE: Inside, maybe. To rest a spell.

RUTH: I feel sick.

BOONE: Has anyone ever talked to you about moderation?

RUTH: No.

BOONE: It's a talk I would recommend. As we age, we develop moderation. Otherwise we would jump off the edge and die. It's why I said a little cake.

RUTH: I might puke.

BOONE: Well that would not surprise Boone. I've seen what hunger can do.

RUTH: What can hunger do?

BOONE: It destroys the human urge for moderation. It makes us animals. Extreme.

RUTH: I am extreme.

BOONE: I know you are, baby.

RUTH: Excuse me.

Ruth pukes in the dirt.

BOONE: There, baby.

Ruth pukes. Boone holds her head.

BOONE (CONT): There.

Ruth rests. Boone stands.

BOONE (CONT): Come rinse your mouth with a little lemonade.

RUTH: I'm sorry.

BOONE: You been working so long.

RUTH: This wheat makes me sick.

BOONE: That's not the wheat, baby. It's your desire.

Ruth pukes and pukes. Boone watches from the porch.

BOONE (CONT): No one ever told you to eat the whole thing.

Four

After sunrise. Ruth sleeps on the porch. Sugar enters.

SUGAR: Tonight's the night.

RUTH: You found me.

SUGAR: Go to him.

RUTH: I can't.

SUGAR: Harvest is ending and everything's gonna turn. Tonight Boone goes to the threshing floor to beat the useful from the waste. Gonna do it himself. He'll start at quitting time and work till he falls. Sweat and sores and good clean wheat. Then you creep to this pile of a man and loosen his boots. The relief will wake him, but you just shhh. Hold his feet in your belly, his feet in your thighs. Melt yourself into the creased places. Sing him a resting song. He will sleep like a growing thing. He will wake and never leave you.

RUTH: That's how it works, huh.

SUGAR: Baby…

RUTH: I was throwing up all yesterday just hearing that word.

SUGAR: You threw up from the sweets. It's not natural. A whole cake. Now there is a tall tale. There is a tale for my grandkids. Ruthie and the whole cake.

Sugar starts to laugh.

RUTH: Don't laugh at me. I miss you so much my body won't work. It's not a tall tale.

SUGAR: Where are you, Ruth? I want to touch your face.

RUTH: I'm here.

SUGAR: You been crying. That's not right.

RUTH: No.

SUGAR: You are an exquisite child. You make my breath skip. Like a baby sleeping in the day.

RUTH: I usually wake up early.

SUGAR: I know you do. We have been admiring your strength.

RUTH: You have?

SUGAR: He tells me every morning what you have on and how much you carry.

RUTH: You keep track of me?

SUGAR: He likes you.

RUTH: Stop it.

SUGAR: You know half this farm was mine? Boone said we could buy it back anytime. But now he won't sell.

RUTH: Is that because you're broke?

SUGAR: When I am restored to my own place, I can make tough decisions. For now I am a guest in Boone's house. A man who's been waiting to sour my luck. He likes you.

RUTH: I won't do it.

SUGAR: I wish for you a baby. My babies are the one thing that never went wrong.

RUTH: No?

SUGAR: I wish for you simple love. Regeneration.

RUTH: What if I don't want a baby?

SUGAR: A woman is only a woman for so many years. She then becomes a neutral thing. This has certain advantages, such as safety on a road or in a field. But in general it is a painful time. A time for loss. I have lost so many things. I used to make rich meals from my mother's recipes. I have lost those cards. I don't know how to do anything anymore. Not even see.

RUTH: You will never be a neutral thing.

SUGAR: Ruth. I can't give you any results.

RUTH: I just want to hold right now.

SUGAR: I'm going to die.

RUTH: I'll go. Stop it. I'll go. Please stop.

Five

The threshing floor. Late, late night. Boone flails the wheat and sings.

BOONE:
A shake-a split-a beat my wheat.
A shake-a split-a beat my wheat.
You got your good side
You got your bad side
I give you separation sweet.

Now here I got a stack a grain.
And here I got a load a pain.
I shake my old tools
I break your new rules
I split the body from the brain.

Now here I got a man who's smart.
A bin for head and one for heart.
No painful mixture
That's how he fixed her
The whole can take a man apart.

A shake-a split-a beat my wheat
A break-a sweat in all this heat
A rake the bitter from the sweet.

BOONE (CONT): *A shake-a split-a --*

Boone drops the flail mid-stroke and falls into the straw, asleep. Ruth enters and watches him a while. She loosens his boots.

RUTH: Man's got to rest.

BOONE: Sugar?

RUTH: Let me think up a song.

BOONE:

In dreams.

Used to be two men a boy and a horse could thresh a whole crop ... then big machine... ring a men... Pay was the wife's best beef dinner... Now two men a combine no boy no horse... farmer set on his porch and figure. Sugar when you coming home?

Boone falls back asleep.

RUTH: Wake up. I'm soothing you.

She takes off his boots and rubs his feet, awkwardly semi-singing:

You don't have to work by night. You are a rich man.
You don't have to work your back. You are an old man.

BOONE: Used to be, used to be.

RUTH: You shh.
You are a rich old man.
And it's all gonna be fine.

Ruth holds his bare feet in her belly. Boone wakes up.

BOONE: Oh my.

RUTH: *You are a rich old man.*
And it's all gonna be fine.

BOONE: Look who's here.

RUTH: I don't really sing. I can fuck pretty good though, if you like.

Boone starts to laugh.

RUTH (CONT): Why does everyone laugh at me?

BOONE: Because you are funny. Lay down next to Boone.

RUTH: Okay.

BOONE: Sugar send you?

RUTH: I don't know.

BOONE: You're just a little thing.

RUTH: I'm thirty years old and pretty strong.

BOONE: You act like a tiny girl.

RUTH: Does that mean you don't want to fuck me?

BOONE: Course I do, child, but time has an effect. We know all about your loyalty and kind deeds. And here you offer yourself to an old man. That's a rare kind of compassion, no matter how much land I got. You're doing right by your mother. Now rest.

RUTH: I can't sleep.

BOONE: Try counting all the endings to your life.

RUTH: Hit the road, own a farm, fall into the sea.

BOONE: What a sleepy girl.

Sings:

You can lie back
I will rock you.
You can go limp
I will hold you.
My arms are stronger than you think.
Strong as the spring
You can do nothing and know

BOONE (CONT): *You'll never sink*
Or even stay still.

RUTH: I'm supposed to do that.

Ruth falls asleep in Boone's arms. Boone sleeps.
Time passes.

BOONE: Child. Child. Leave the barn before
it gets light.

RUTH: What do I tell Sugar?

BOONE: Take her what clean grain you can
carry.

RUTH: I can carry a lot.

BOONE: Take it all.

RUTH: Thank you. Thank you.

Ruth gathers a huge amount of grain and exits.

BOONE: Surprise. New day for Boone.
Surprise.

Six

Minutes later. Sugar is paring fruit on the porch.
Ruth tries to walk by with the grain.

SUGAR: Baby.

RUTH: Morning.

SUGAR: Heard your step.

RUTH: You're working.

SUGAR: I better start earning our keep.

RUTH: I work.

SUGAR: You carry half what a man can and he
knows it.
Did you have a nice visit?

RUTH: He's a good person. He gave us all
this.

Sugar feels the grain.

SUGAR: I pick right.

RUTH: Mmm hmm.

SUGAR: The man deserves pleasure.

RUTH: It wasn't that kind of a night.

SUGAR: I taste your skin in my sleep.

RUTH: So wake up.

Ruth takes Sugar in her arms.

SUGAR: Watch the knife.

RUTH: I got you.

Sugar kisses Ruth hard on the mouth.

SUGAR: Is it night?

RUTH: Broad day.

SUGAR: Oh.

RUTH: I'll take you inside.

SUGAR: We will be missed.

RUTH: I don't care.

SUGAR: That Boone could kick us off his land.

Ruth lets go of Sugar.

RUTH: You can tell time. Why do you kiss me now, at dawn, when work starts?

SUGAR: I'm frightened.

RUTH: You know where I sleep.

Ruth exits. Sugar feels the grain.

Seven

Minutes later. The threshing floor. Boone sleeps in the straw.

Ruth enters and watches him a while.

She unbuttons her shirt.

RUTH: Wake up.

Boone smiles and mutters, sleepy. He opens his eyes, turns around, sees Ruth.

They regard each other in silence.

Boone lunges for Ruth and pulls her down.

They devour each other in the straw.

Eight

Colder weather. Sugar stands on the porch. Noon.

SUGAR: DINNER! GET YOUR DINNER!

Boone strolls in.

BOONE: You had an active morning.

SUGAR: Gotta match your active nights.

BOONE: What'd you make me?

SUGAR: What you making for me?

BOONE: Some things are private.

SUGAR: Uh huh. Come eat the first roast beef of my late life.

BOONE: How you know it's done?

SUGAR: I drank the juice and didn't taste blood. Where's your lady?

BOONE: Working.

Ruth enters in loose pants.

RUTH: Get me a towel.

BOONE and SUGAR: Yes ma'am.

RUTH: Boone, honey, would you get that towel?

Boone trots off.

SUGAR: I roasted you a roast.

RUTH: I can't keep that down.

SUGAR: You need some nourishment.

RUTH: Boone cooks me bone broth every night and spreads out the marrow on toast. I enjoy that.

SUGAR: Do you show?

Ruth places Sugar's hand on her belly.

Mmm.

Ruth moves Sugar's hand to her breast.

RUTH: Don't I feel nice?

SUGAR: I used to lie home and watch my body curve.

RUTH: Well you're pretty lazy. I like to work.

Boone enters with a tall pile of clean towels.

BOONE: Towel for my sweaty filly! Twenty clean towels right here.

SUGAR: You are a wastrel.

BOONE: Thresherman's towels. From when we drew a crowd. Those dinners were something. A man could eat his way through a twenty foot table and still leave room for a pie.

RUTH: Do we have pie?

SUGAR: You gave up sweets.

RUTH: Why give up?

BOONE: Now when I say a pie, I don't mean a hand-held pint-size tart. I mean a wheel of fruit or cream or nuts or all three together. Lemon berry, pecan pear, cherry almond cheese. I will describe the other pies when I have your attention. Meantime, wipe your head.

SUGAR: I remember one dinner when the threshermen came to our farm. I angled to wait on you, Boone.

BOONE: And you got my brother.

SUGAR: So like, one to the other. Two of you a teenage dream. When one went swimming the other got wet. Imagine her joy when you were both born.

BOONE: We going to eat or talk?

SUGAR: Well I can't drag a hot roast out to this porch without burning the both of you. It's wintertime. Aren't you cold?

RUTH: Love can do marvelous things.

SUGAR: I am happy for you but I don't plan to freeze.

Sugar holds out her hand for Boone's arm.

BOONE: You okay?

RUTH: Starving as a thresherman who missed his breakfast.

BOONE: I like how you eat. Come on.

RUTH: Just give me a minute to breathe in the clean.

Boone leads Sugar inside. Ruth vomits into a towel.

Nine

Hard rain. Night. Boone and Sugar sit on the
porch with a thermos of coffee and a bottle of scotch.
Boone sings an old song.

BOONE:
Oh rose rose rose, I'd break a thorn for you.
My love it grows like weeds and children do.
I left my heart in
your daddy's garden
Oh rose rose rose, keep it beating true.

SUGAR: Faster.

Boone sings it again, faster. Sugar claps along.

Faster.

Boone sings the song very fast. Sugar claps him on.

Faster.

Boone sings a blur. Llaughs and laughs.

SUGAR: You got a voice that stays with a
person.

BOONE: We ought to go in.

SUGAR: The one where you throw the stick.
Do that one. Throw the stick.

BOONE: You're crazy.

SUGAR: You throw the stick and you hop the fence and you swing from the top of a tree. Do that one.

BOONE: Ready?

SUGAR: Ready.

BOONE:
I throw the stick, I hop the fence, I swing from the top of the tree.
Whoo hoo! Here I am. Swinging from the top of the tree.
Whoo hoo! Watch me fly. Flying from the top of the tree.

SUGAR: You climb like you grew from the top down. Magical boy full of pockets and songs. Watch you swing and kick.

BOONE: It is so right to swap stories with you.

SUGAR: Go Boone, go!

A loud scream from inside the house. Quiet.

SUGAR (CONT): Rain's good.

BOONE: Uh huh.

SUGAR: Gonna be a fine year.

BOONE: What if the crop molds?

Another, louder scream.

SUGAR: It won't.

BOONE: I ought to go in.

SUGAR: Let her keep some dignity. Now how do you prevent the wheat from going bad?

BOONE: Timing. The more water, the better crop. But -- the more water, the more danger. You want it to ripen but not soak. You just reap a little early if it's a wet year. You just balance it out.

A ragged series of screams.

SUGAR: Tell me about the threshing ring.

BOONE: One time we were threshing down there at old Billy's, you know, and it was hot. And Billy wanted to blow some oat straw into the barn. And we had an awful time getting the machine set up to blow the straw in the barn there. I was just wringing wet with sweat, and it was steaming anyhow. And this boy name of Earl come out and he jumped up on the engine box there and set down beside me and he said, "Well, if it's any hotter in hell then it is in there," he said, "there ain't no use to send me down cause I can't stand it."

Sugar and Boone laugh. More screams. Sugar and Boone drink.

Ten

A sunny day. Sugar nurses the baby.

SUGAR: Now don't you pull so tight. I'm out of practice. He's gonna be a biter, I can tell already. You know the kind who set in with their jaw from day one, taking all they can get, bearing down hard. He's gonna be a fighter. Aren't you? Aren't you? Easy now, Sugar's got to learn it all again. You know there's no talking to men. Even tiny ones. They just pull and bite, suck you deep. But then they draw wet you thought was dry. Glory be. A baby. Me with milk. I have always loved this farm.
You want to see his pee-pee? Come close, I don't want to chill him. Gather round, I'm going to open the blanket. There. You want to touch it? Go on, they don't remember. Go on. Nice, huh?

You want to kiss it? Go on. Go on. Well I'm not afraid of a little skin.

She kisses it.

SUGAR (CONT): Sweet sweet boy. Sweet glory boy.

Again, longer.

SUGAR (CONT): May you grow into a black-haired horse.

Boone enters.

BOONE: What witchery are you committing on my son?

SUGAR: Just showing the people his parts. You resting up?

BOONE: I smoked so many damn cigars I can't breathe.

SUGAR: We know how to celebrate.

Ruth steps out onto the porch in her men's shoes, with her bag.

BOONE: Now wrap him up. He has to nurse.

SUGAR: I'm nursing, Boone. Watch. I am nursing.

Boone watches

BOONE: Yes. You are nursing my child.

Ruth steps off the porch.

SUGAR: Is it you?

RUTH: I was not afraid of the birth. At night beside the road you opened around my whole hand and I felt your heart beat. I thought, we can hold anything. We can stretch without pain. It's not true. I thought of you and my hand the whole time. It didn't work.

You'll never let me do that again, will you? Will you?

I don't want to know his name.

Don't tell him mine.

Keep him warm. Keep him safe. If that's possible.

Tell him, you are a child of desire. You better watch what you want.

Ruth walks away without looking back.

SUGAR: Your mother had a way of saying the truth that put other people to shame. She stayed by me when everyone was gone. She touched me and I stopped hating myself. She led me home and stood beside me and I said, everyone is gone. I am so grateful. I am so ashamed.

I am going to drop this baby, Boone.

Boone takes the baby. Silence. Boone sings his lullaby.

BOONE:

You can lie back
I will rock you.
You can go limp
I will hold you.
My arms are stronger than you think
Strong as the spring.
You can do nothing and know
You'll never sink
Or even stay still.

You can grow up
I will watch you.
You can leave home
I will love you.
My heart is bigger than I know
Big as the sea
So run as far as you can go
You'll always be
A child of my own.

End of Part Two

Epilogue

Orpah stands in a spotlight before a microphone in a glamorous red dress and gloves. Thunderous applause.

ORPAH: Thank you. Thank you, every one.
Your appreciation is my wide world.
I can't see you all past these radiant lights, but I can hear your applause and it is like thunder.
Like gunfire. Like a big big cannon keeping this country safe.
I can't tell you how good it feels that so many of you chose me tonight. Are you ready for my song?

Orpah leans into the microphone as if to sing, then pulls back and speaks.

Let me hear it again, boys. The big big sound of your love.

Loud applause and cheers.

You, and you, and you are my hero.
Remember *that* when times get tight. It's not just your sweethearts and your mothers and your wives. It's girls like me that belong to no man who will pray all night for your safe return.
I've been working extra hard on my song.

Again almost begins, then pulls back.

ORPAH (CONT): Do I look pretty to you?

Some girls believe in mystery but Miss Orpah will tell you straight. I've been working extra hard on my looks. I want to be so beautiful for you. Am I?

Enthusiastic response.

Ooh. I'm in a little bit of pain.

She removes one stiletto pump to the delight of the crowd, shakes it, and slips it back on.

A tiny stone. Now see another girl might dance on top of that all night and just bite her smile a bit but it's not in my nature to fake. Anything.

Big response.

That's right. You gonna remember me?

Crowd roars.

You're not gonna just disappear like some?

Big hollers of "no."

You're gonna come on back, right?

Crowd roars. She whispers.

ORPAH (CONT): Come on back.

Lights get harsh. The dress looks cheap. Loud stripper music. Orpah strips and sings.

I'm a lonely girl
Never seen the world
My body is the only place I know.
I'm the only girl
Remaining in my world
You're driving me as far as I can go.

Orpah stands in a spotlight wearing enough to be legal.

Mmmm. That's as far as I go boys. How I would like to show you the very last bit. You'll just have to come home safe and see. Good night.

Orpah blows a kiss. Pause.

Thank you. I do enjoy the attention, I'm not ashamed to say. Thank you, every one. I will miss you, every one. Good night.

Orpah blows another kiss. Pause.

CAN WE BRING THE LIGHTS DOWN PLEASE?

Got to leave a little mystery. We're not supposed to walk off in the light.

Crowd gets louder.

ORPAH (CONT): PLEASE?
Got to keep you guessing. We're not supposed
to turn our backs on the crowd.
FADE ME OUT **NOW!**
Well. Go on home, gentlemen. I'm dressing.

Orpah hoists the dress onto her body.

Which one of you boys is going to zip me up?

*Ruth steps into Orpah's light, wearing men's sailor
whites. She slowly zips the dress, then kneels to
pick up each shoe and brush out the stones before
slipping them onto Orpah's feet.*

RUTH: I know how you hate to be
uncomfortable.

ORPAH: You pay attention.

RUTH: Yes I do.

ORPAH: That's better than ninety nine point
nine percent of mankind.

RUTH: Do you ever keep your clothes on when
you dance?

ORPAH: In private.

RUTH: I would like that.

Ruth and Orpah dance.

ORPAH: Do I know you?

RUTH: I... I...

ORPAH: I knew a girl who stuttered that way.

RUTH: It's not a stutter. I think out loud.

ORPAH: Come here.

Orpah holds Ruth's face. The stage lights flash on and off wildly.

ORPAH (CONT): HENRY GO HOME! YOU GO ON HOME! I WILL KILL YOU TOMORROW FOR WHAT YOU DID TO ME! GO ON NOW! GO!

The lights go to pitch black.

ORPAH (CONT): Ruth.

RUTH: SHHHH.

ORPAH: You got a match?

RUTH: Somewhere.

ORPAH: Thinks he's God cause he's by the light. He's not God. YOU'RE NOT GOD HENRY! YOU'RE JUST A FAT VULGAR MAN! NOT EVEN A MAN! A PECKERLESS FAKE!

Ruth strikes the match.

ORPAH: Oh. Not to say that... Oh my.

Orpah begins to laugh.

RUTH: Pecker-less...

Ruth begins to laugh. They laugh hard together. The match burns Ruth's hand.

RUTH: OW.

Ruth blows out the match.

ORPAH: Light another one.

RUTH: Don't you have a candle?

ORPAH: Probably. Light another one so I can see.

Ruth lights another match.

ORPAH: That's nice.

RUTH: Get the candle.

Orpah finds a piece of candle. Ruth lights it.

ORPAH: Well aren't we a drugstore romance?

RUTH: You sing well.

ORPAH: Think I could make it?

RUTH: I do.

ORPAH: Want to come down the coast and help start my career?

RUTH: I ship out tomorrow.

ORPAH: How come you picked her?

RUTH: Love.

ORPAH: Hah.

RUTH: Yeah. Hah.

ORPAH: Woman didn't even like you.

RUTH: She went blind. That helped a little.

ORPAH: I guess it would.

RUTH: How about you?

ORPAH: Oh, I'm a solo act. I will always make the solitary choice. I guess that's just part of being a woman with a goal.

RUTH: I've seen a lot of kindness between people.

ORPAH: You're lucky.

RUTH: I still imagine her.

ORPAH: That's natural.

RUTH: I want to visit when I come home. Her. This nice man Boone. My son.

ORPAH: How old is your boy?

RUTH: Seven years eight months and nineteen days.

ORPAH: Oh.

RUTH: What's wrong with that?

ORPAH: I'm pregnant.

RUTH: Oh.

ORPAH: May not be fancy as blindness, but it's true.

RUTH: I believe you.

ORPAH: So at the risk of turning long odds into humiliation, will you accompany me down the coast?

RUTH: On the farm I would dream that I was peeking through a row of wheat and the furrow filled with water and I stepped in and rode it like a river out to sea.

ORPAH: Aren't we all some kind of joke.

RUTH: I don't think it's funny.

ORPAH: That's because you have no sense of humor, Ruth.

RUTH: True.

Silence. Ruth and Orpah burst out laughing.

ORPAH: Look at you, sailor. Look at you.

RUTH: Do you think we can ever go back and pick up all the pieces and people we let go?

ORPAH: You're here, right?

RUTH: Yes.

Silence.

ORPAH: Did you come find me, or were you just walking by?

Quiet.

That's okay. You're here, right?

RUTH: I'm here.

ORPAH: I used to think about your loyalty a lot. At night, riding in the back of a truck on top of the rocks in the road, I would toss around and then imagine you, walking over those same stones. I would fall asleep thinking of courage, and kindness.

RUTH: I began to believe that family was a thing I could pick like fruit. She wanted a son.

ORPAH: You were better to her than seven sons.

RUTH: Sometimes I feel like a bundle of loss.

ORPAH: I don't think that's who we are, Ruth. It's what we carry.

RUTH: I hope so.

ORPAH: I want you to take your bundle out to sea and drop it like a stone.

RUTH: Splash.

Ocean sounds begin.

ORPAH: I'm going to call this baby David.

RUTH: David?

ORPAH: He knew how to handle stones.

Ruth hurls an imaginary stone.

ORPAH (CONT): You are something else.

RUTH: I am. I am something else.

Ruth walks into the light, into the sea.

End of Play

Notes on Contributors

KAREN HARTMAN is the award-winning author of twenty plays and musical works including *Goliath* (Dorothy Silver Playwriting Prize); *Gum, Leah's Train, Going Gone* (N.E.A. New Play Grant); *Anatomy 1968; ALICE: Tales of a Curious Girl* (Music by Gina Leishman, AT&T Onstage Award); *Troy Women; Donna Wants; Sea Change*, a musical with score by AnnMarie Milazzo, and *MotherBone*, an opera composed by Graham Reynolds (Frederick Loewe Award for New Music Theater). Her work been performed in New York at the Women's Project, NAATCO, P73, the NY Fringe, and Summer Play Festival, and at regional theaters including Center Stage, Cincinnati Playhouse, the Magic Theater, Dallas Theater Center, and elsewhere. Her other plays are published by Theater Communications Group, Dramatists Play Service, Playscripts, Backstage Books, and NoPassport Press. She has received new play commissions from ACT in San Francisco, California Shakespeare Festival, McCarter Theater, La Jolla Playhouse, South Coast Repertory, and others. An alumna of New Dramatists and Yale (B.A., M.F.A.), her work has been supported by the Rockefeller Foundation at Bellagio, the N.E.A., the Helen Merrill Foundation, the Vogelstein Foundation, a Daryl Roth "Creative Spirit" Award, a Hodder Fellowship, a Jerome Fellowship, a Fulbright Scholarship to Jerusalem, and Core Membership at the Playwrights Center. Ms. Hartman has taught playwriting extensively, including several years at the Yale School of Drama, and currently leads independent workshops in New York.

JEAN RANDICH has been directing new work and re-imagining the classics for over twenty years. She has directed world premieres of plays, operas, and musicals by Karen Hartman, Catherine Filloux, Jeffrey M. Jones, Len Jenkin and Art Spiegelman, among others. She has worked extensively in New York and in regional theaters. Ms. Randich has also directed in Germany and Norway. She was commissioned by the Dallas Opera to write the libretto for a chamber opera, *The Miraculous Phonograph Record* and co-wrote the book and lyrics of the musical, *The Unknown*. Ms. Randich has received an NEA/TCG Director Fellowship, a Fox Foundation Grant to work at the National Theatre in Oslo, Norway, and a Jonathan Larson Performing Arts Grant. She holds a Masters in Creative Writing from Brown University and a Master of Fine Arts from the Yale School of Drama. Ms. Randich is currently on the faculties of Bennington College and NYU.

More titles from NoPassport Press

Antigone Project: A Play in Five Parts

by Tanya Barfield, Karen Hartman, Chiori Miyagawa, Lynn Nottage and Caridad Svich, with preface by Lisa Schlesinger, introduction by Marianne McDonald; **ISBN 978-0-578-03150-7**

Amparo Garcia-Crow: The South Texas Plays

(Cocks Have Claws and Wings to Fly, Under a Western Sky, The Faraway Nearby, Esmeralda Blue) **Preface by Octavio Solis**
ISBN: 978-0-578-01913-0

Anne Garcia-Romero: Collected Plays

(Earthquake Chica, Santa Concepcion, Mary Peabody in Cuba)
Preface by Juliette Carrillo
ISBN: 978-0-6151-8888-1

John Jesurun: Deep Sleep, White Water, Black Maria –

A Media Trilogy Preface by Fiona Templeton
ISBN: 978-0-578-02602-2

Lorca: Six Major Plays

(Blood Wedding, Dona Rosita, The House of Bernarda Alba, The Public, The Shoemaker's Prodigious Wife, Yerma)
In new translations by Caridad Svich, Preface by James Leverett, introduction by Amy Rogoway;
ISBN: 978-0-578-00221-7

Matthew Maguire: Three Plays

(The Tower, Luscious Music, The Desert) **Preface by Naomi Wallace;**

ISBN: 978-0-578-00856-1

Oliver Mayer: Collected Plays

(Conjunto, Joe Louis Blues, Ragged Time) **Preface by Luis Alfaro,**

Introduction by Jon D. Rossini;

ISBN: 978-0-6151-8370-1

Alejandro Morales: Collected Plays

(expat/inferno, marea, Sebastian);

ISBN: 978-0-6151-8621-4

12 Ophelias (a play with broken songs) by Caridad Svich

ISBN: 978-0-6152-4918-6

NoPassport is a sponsored project of Fractured Atlas, a non-profit arts service organization. Contributions in behalf of [Caridad Svich & NoPassport] may be made payable to Fractured Atlas and are tax-deductible to the extent permitted by law.

For online donations go directly to
https://www.fracturedatlas.org/donate/2623

www.ingramcontent.com/pod-product-compliance
Lightning Source LLC
Chambersburg PA
CBHW030346030726
47499CB00003B/922